PAMELA
DUNCAN EDWARDS

ILLUSTRATED BY
HENRY COLE

*Dutton
Children's
Books*

The Old House

FOR HAZEL, TIM, HENRY, AND ALEX WHO FELL IN LOVE WITH *THEIR* "OLD HOUSE" AND MADE IT THEIR OWN—**PDE**

FOR CAROLYN, WITH LOVE—**HC**

DUTTON CHILDREN'S BOOKS

A division of Penguin Young Readers Group

PUBLISHED BY THE PENGUIN GROUP

Penguin Group (USA) Inc., 375 Hudson Street, New York, New York 10014, U.S.A. • Penguin Group (Canada), 90 Eglinton Avenue East, Suite 700, Toronto, Ontario, Canada M4P 2Y3 (a division of Pearson Penguin Canada Inc.) • Penguin Books Ltd, 80 Strand, London WC2R 0RL, England • Penguin Ireland, 25 St Stephen's Green, Dublin 2, Ireland (a division of Penguin Books Ltd) • Penguin Group (Australia), 250 Camberwell Road, Camberwell, Victoria 3124, Australia (a division of Pearson Australia Group Pty Ltd) • Penguin Books India Pvt Ltd, 11 Community Centre, Panchsheel Park, New Delhi - 110 017, India • Penguin Group (NZ), 67 Apollo Drive, Rosedale, North Shore 0745, Auckland, New Zealand (a division of Pearson New Zealand Ltd) • Penguin Books (South Africa) (Pty) Ltd, 24 Sturdee Avenue, Rosebank, Johannesburg 2196, South Africa • Penguin Books Ltd, Registered Offices: 80 Strand, London WC2R 0RL, England

Library of Congress Cataloging-in-Publication Data

Edwards, Pamela Duncan.

The old house / by Pamela Duncan Edwards ; illustrated by Henry Cole. — 1st ed.

p. cm.

Summary: An old empty house feels sorry for itself because it has no family living inside, but with the help of some good friends, its dreams come true.

ISBN 978-0-525-47796-9 (alk. paper)

[1. Friendship—Fiction. 2. Home—Fiction.] I. Cole, Henry, date- ill. II. Title.

PZ7.E26365Ol 2007 [E]—dc22 2006102950

Published in the United States by Dutton Children's Books, a division of Penguin Young Readers Group, 345 Hudson Street, New York, New York 10014 www.penguin.com/youngreaders

Designed by Heather Wood • Manufactured in China • First Edition

1 3 5 7 9 10 8 6 4 2

*O*nce upon a time,
there was an old house.

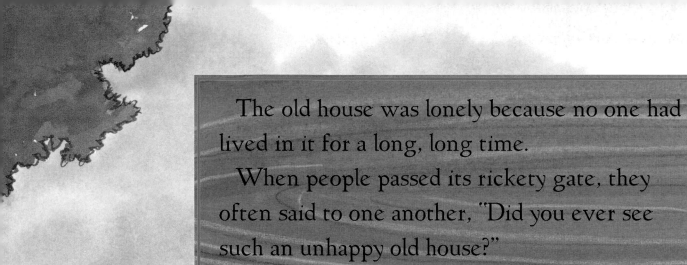

The old house was lonely because no one had lived in it for a long, long time.

When people passed its rickety gate, they often said to one another, "Did you ever see such an unhappy old house?"

Its friends tried to cheer it up.
"You're so useful," chattered the birds.
"Your eaves are perfect for our nests."

"You're helpful, too," said the squirrel. "You always remember where I hid my nuts."

"Your yard is exactly right for us," agreed the wildflowers. "It's so pretty. What would we all do without you?"

"We love you, no matter what," whispered the oak tree, wrapping its twiggy arms around the roof of the old house.

"It doesn't do any good feeling sorry for yourself," they cried.

But it was no use. "I'm so empty inside," sobbed the old house.

Sometimes people came to look around the old house. But they always went away again.

"You'd have to be crazy to want to live in such an old heap," said one couple. "Even if it is reduced in price."

"WHAT?!" cried the old house in a horrified voice. "I've been REDUCED?"

Its window shutters drooped in disgust.

REDUCED!

"The only thing to do with that dump is to knock it down," a man sneered.

When it heard these words, the old house cried so hard that its timbers became damp and musty. It began to ache in all its joints. Even its friends shivered in fright.

One day a family stopped by the rickety gate.

"Oh!" said the mother. "I've always dreamed of living in a quaint old place like this."

"We've never lived in a real house," said the boy. "Could we just go and look at it?"

Just then the old house gave one of its big, sorrowful sighs.

"Uh-oh!" said the father. "I think it might have rot."

"No!" cried the little girl. "It's just saying hello to us, that's all."

"Hey," the squirrel whispered to the old house. "Did you hear that? This is your big chance!"

But the old house sniffed. "Look! They're going away like all the others," it whined.

But the next week the family appeared again. They stared at the house longingly.

"I'd put a tire swing up there," said the boy, gazing at the oak.

"Look at the nests," said the mother. "This house certainly shares itself with its friends."

"I'd pull the grass from around the wildflowers," said the girl. "Then they'd be able to get to the light."

"Do you think the house is leaning sideways?" asked the father. "I wonder if its foundation is cracked."

"EXCUSE ME!" cried the old house indignantly. "My foundation is NOT cracked!"

"Then stop sagging!" said the squirrel. "Stand tall!"

"Get a grip on yourself," urged the oak tree. "Twinkle your windows!"

"Think how disappointed they're going to be!" twittered the birds.

"You can do it!" whispered the wildflowers.

The old house looked at the wishful face
of the mother and the uncertain face of the
father. It saw the eager faces of the boy and
the girl, and it heard the baby gurgle.

This family needs me, thought the old house, and it took a deep breath.

It wriggled and
stretched and pushed
with all its might,
until it stood as
straight as possible.

"It's not leaning at all," said the boy.

"You're right," said the father. "A shadow must have fallen across it for a minute."

The girl looked at her mother and father. "Could we buy it?" she asked.

"We've been saving money for a house, but it would take a lot of work to fix this one," said the mother.

"It certainly would," said the father.

Then the family started walking away.

"STOP! DON'T GO!" cried the old house.
"We could be so happy together."
But the family was gone.

The old house was miserable. "I could have been their home," it mourned. "I could have kept them safe and warm."

"Have you noticed that it feels sad for the family?" the squirrel whispered to the oak tree. "It's stopped feeling sorry for itself."

"I know," answered the oak tree. "That's *one* good thing, at least."

One morning, a rumbling noise came from down the lane.

"IT'S THE BULLDOZER!" wailed the old house. "This is the end! We're doomed!"

"Who'll save our nests?" screeched the birds. "Our babies can't fly yet."

"They'll trample us flat," cried the wildflowers.

"I know they'll chop me down, too," groaned the oak tree. "Good-bye, old house. You've been a good friend."

They all creaked and rustled and squawked and trembled in terror.

But suddenly the old house stopped shivering.

"Hey!" it exclaimed. "Look! It's not the bulldozer. IT'S MY FAMILY!"

And it was!

The mother washed the windows of the old house until they flashed like diamonds. She painted the frames a sparkling white.

The father hammered in new pieces of wood, and baby birds watched as he mended holes in the roof.

"All my aches and pains are going away!" cried the old house.

While the boy swung from the oak tree, the squirrel played peekaboo with the baby.

The girl pulled up grass around the wild-flowers so they could feel the warm sun. She sprinkled seeds on the ground for the birds to eat.

The family worked so hard that the old house began to feel young again.

And if the old house ever creaked, it did so from joy and not from sadness. For it was so filled with laughter and love that people passing its rickety gate often said to one another:

"Did you ever see such a happy old house?"